Mariella Mystery
Investigates

The Disappearance of Diana Dumpling

Never miss a clue!

Join our **Mariella Mystery Investigates Club** for the latest news on your favorite sleuth-y detective, plus:

- A club certificate and membership card
- **Mariella Mystery** games, activities, puzzles, and coloring pages
- Excerpts from the books and news about forthcoming titles
- Contests for **FREE** stuff

You can become the next Young Super Sleuth—just like Mariella!

Visit **barronsbooks.com/mariella/** today and join in the fun!

Open to U.S. residents only.

Certificate

This is to certify that

_____

is an official member in good standing of

Mariella Mystery
Investigates Club

and entitled to all rights & privileges

granted this _____ day of _____

Look out for more books about Mariella Mystery

The Spaghetti Yeti
The Kitty Calamity
The Ghostly Guinea Pig
A Cupcake Conundrum
The Huge Hair Scare
The Curse of the Pampered Poodle

Mariella Mystery

Investigates

The Disappearance of Diana Dumpling

by Kate Pankhurst

BARRON'S

For my school lunch buddies—
Fi, Jen, and Nic

BE STEALTH. LIKE A SHADOW!

CLUES! CLUES! clues

hat

Me, wearing my badge.

Woof! Woof! Beep!

SUPER POWERED SNIFFER CIRCUITS

6

THIS YOUNG SUPER SLEUTH
JOURNAL BELONGS TO ...

Mariella Mystery, that's me! Totally
amazing girl detective, aged nine
and three quarters.

I'm so good at solving mysteries, I think
it's about time I won an award—that's
why I've awarded myself an Official
Mega-Mystery-Girl Badge of Honor.

(NOTE: If you are thinking of
making another attempt to
steal my badge, Arthur,
don't bother. There's
no way I'll slip up and
leave it on my dress in
the hamper again.)

BADGE

MEGA MYSTERY GIRL

The Puddleford Elementary School Presents...

Princess and the Pea

Parents are invited to the performance in the school auditorium,

Friday, May 22nd 12 PM

Is she a real princess? The only way to find out is to see if she gets a wink of sleep lying on a pea plucked from the vegetable patch at Puddleford Elementary.

STARRING ★
PRIMROSE
PARRINSON

PEA

WARNING: Contains silly songs about peas and lots of dancing. (Not how professional detectives spend their time, but there was no getting out of it.)

Pick me!

Sunday May 17th

Mariella

violet

Poppy

NOTE: Mom has finished knitting our string bean costumes (she runs an online knitting shop called Knitted Fancies (You Name It, We'll Knit it.) Even though these look quite silly, we might need them if a mystery involving vegetable theft occurs.

yarn

mystery HQ →

3:30 PM
MYSTERY GIRL HQ
(TREEHOUSE IN MY YARD)

This afternoon's incident shows that I can't afford
to let my Mystery Senses tune out, not even for a
moment.

CASE REPORT: OPERATION CONVINCING STRING BEAN UPDATE

1:30 PM: Poppy has made us rehearse our
entrance on stage seven times—tiptoeing across
HQ and finishing with a little heel kick and
hand wave. (Apparently if a string bean came
to life, it would totally act like this.)

tiptoe

heel kick

Poppy Holmes: Mystery girl with amazing acting talents. We don't have any lines in the play, so Poppy says we should dedicate our time to becoming Masters of Disguise. She said if we can be convincing string beans, we can pretend to be anything.

POPPY with a string bean

Violet on the mystery beanbag.

Violet Maple: Totally cool Mystery Girl. Pleased Poppy and I can support her through her stage fright. (I've told her she has nothing to be worried about because we've been in mystery situations far more dramatic than a play about a pea.)

I'm alive!

Mariella Mystery
(me): Mystery is what I do, that's why I'm a Mystery Girl. Master-of-Disguise training might be useful in the future, but I'd prefer a real and dramatic mystery to solve.

me, at the mystery desk.

1:45 PM: Poppy tells me and Violet to continue practicing while she goes to the bathroom or we'll never be convincing string beans, just three girls jumping around in green tights.

1:47 PM: Poppy bursts back into HQ, performing a new move. Violet and I try to follow but we can't keep up. Poppy runs around in circles, waving her hands and knocking things over. This definitely doesn't seem like something a string bean would do.

12

1:55 PM: I tell Poppy to slow down. Poppy ignores me, grabs our hands and makes us spin in a circle.

1:59 PM: Violet screams for it to stop and we land in a heap on the floor, but Poppy's legs are a blur of green tights as she kicks them wildly in the air.

2:00 PM: I shout at Poppy that there's no way we'll ever remember all these moves.

2:01 PM: The door to HQ swings open. Poppy appears. She stares at us, shocked.

POPPY?

2:02 PM: I have a terrible realization. The string bean lying next to me, still kicking its legs in the air as if it is being electrocuted, is not Poppy. How did I not notice this string bean was shorter than the real Poppy? The Mystery Girls have been tricked and I know exactly by who!

Arthur doing an annoying dance →

IMPOSTER STRING BEAN: Arthur Mystery. Totally annoying younger brother. He has been cast as a baked potato, but due to his ridiculous phobia of potatoes, he is desperate to switch roles.

2:10 PM: Arthur is finally ejected from HQ and Poppy says this is a huge setback in our practice schedule because she needs to leave early to buy some new green tights. (Arthur has put a hole in hers.)

← hole

2:11 PM: I say this is a huge setback in our detective careers. I didn't immediately detect a false Mystery Girl—there is clearly something very wrong with my Mystery Senses.

2:12 PM: The rest of the Move Like a String Bean practice session is officially canceled.

Spaghetti Bolognese

5:25 PM
MY HOUSE, 22 SYCAMORE AVENUE
(DINNER TIME, SPAGHETTI BOLOGNESE)

Mom and Dad aren't taking what Arthur did seriously at all. Mom says Arthur is feeling uncertain about being a potato in the play and it's making him have emotional outbursts. She says I should be more understanding because I know why he has a phobia of potatoes. Ugh. How could I forget?

Ever since Arthur had an allergic reaction after eating a potato flavored Monster Mash Meal-in-a-Mug* soup, he's refused to eat anything containing potatoes.

itch!
itch!
ARTHUR'S RASH

*MEAL-IN-A-MUG: Instant meal products launched by celebrity children's TV chef, Arabella Flump, two years ago.

Arthur, along with a bunch of other kids, loved them so much that supermarkets struggled to keep up with demand. Unlike Arthur, I had important detective work to do, so couldn't just sit around after school slurping Meal-in-a-Mug like he did.

I had a lucky escape though, because it was revealed that the Meal-in-a-Mug caused terrible allergic reactions. Symptoms included a weird rash, uncontrollable burping, and throwing up. Kids all over the country got sick. The products were instantly banned and Arabella Flump was officially forbidden from working as a chef ever again.

Arthur goes on and on about how overcoming the itchy illness means that he is totally brave enough to become a Mystery Girl. I don't think so. Let's look at the evidence:

EVIDENCE ARTHUR IS NOT CAPABLE OF EVER BEING A MYSTERY GIRL:

A: Arthur is scared of potatoes.
Small, round, non-terrifying vegetables.

↑potatoes

↳wimp

B: He is afraid of the baked potato costume he has to wear in the school play. It's a pillowcase.

C: He is not a girl and we aren't changing the name of our detective agency to the Mystery Girls and a Boy.

I have been so annoyed I totally forgot I have the perfect revenge to use against Arthur!

The other day I was looking for an empty cereal box to make a new fake beard, and I found a leftover multipack of Meal-in-a-Mug! Mom thought she'd thrown

them all away, but they were sitting right at the back of the pantry. I can't wait to see Arthur's face when I tell him they have been touching his Choco Flakes box for months now. Ha!

I'm not going to mention it now, though, not while Mom and Dad are making a final decision about whether I can swap from packed lunches to the amazing new school lunches. Violet and Poppy's parents have already agreed, but that's no good unless I can too. We can't discuss cases if I'm on the Packed Lunch Table and they are on the Hot Lunch Table.

7:15 PM
MY BEDROOM, 22 SYCAMORE AVENUE, MYSTERY
DESK

At last! Mom and Dad delivered their decision and
it's a YES! I'm so pleased I can just about get over
the fact Arthur is switching too. He wants to do
everything I do, which is highly annoying.

I called Poppy and Violet to tell them the good
news. We tried school lunches once before, but that
was when The Big G was in charge, and they were
disgusting.

Vegetable
mush

THE BIG G (AKA MISS
GLENDA BUTTON):
Head Lunch Lady
at Puddleford Elementary.
(Known as the Big G
because she has a BIG
voice that she uses to
shout at people who
refuse to eat her
disgusting specialty dish—Vegetable Mush.)

THE BIG G → Glenda Button

**The Big G and four other lunch ladies have been out
sick for three weeks now, because there has been
an outbreak of Lunch Lady's Finger.***

*LUNCH LADY'S FINGER: An illness commonly
suffered by lunch ladies, because they have
damp hands from washing dishes. The infection
spreads from the hands, causing uncontrollable
itchiness and flaky skin all over the body that
might drop into school lunches. EW! Mom said
she knew a lunch lady who had it once and it
was far worse even than
when Arthur had his
allergic reaction.

flaky
skin

Some new lunch ladies have arrived, from Ladies Who Lunch Agency—and they can cook!

DIANA DUMPLING: Star Lunch Lady, working for Ladies Who Lunch. We already knew Diana because while she was at college studying the Lunch Lady Code of Conduct, she worked in the newsstand on Poppy's street. She said it was her dream to be as successful at lunch-ladying as her mom and grandma, who are both lunch ladies and have published books about school lunch recipes. (The Big G needs to read one.)

Diana Dumpling

Contains RULES

THE LUNCH LADY CODE of CONDUCT

It was an amazing surprise when Diana turned up three weeks ago. Every lunchtime, while she clears tables, we've been having in-depth discussions about mysteries we've solved. (She's totally not just pretending to be interested, like other grown-ups do.)

Everyone is going crazy for a dessert* invented by Diana. It's why the Mystery Girls definitely wanted to swap to hot lunches. I cannot wait to try it tomorrow!

monday munchie Madness

*MONDAY MUNCHIE MADNESS: A chocolate cake served on Mondays that contains hidden healthy ingredients. So it's chocolate and good for you! Roberta Poppet in fourth grade let Violet try some of hers last week. Violet said it tastes like a cloud of chocolate melting in your mouth—she knows stuff about baking and apparently a fluffy chocolate cake like that is really hard to achieve.

MONDAY
May 18th

Saffron
Cauliflower

NOTE: Ladies Who Lunch normally refers to ladies who go out for lunch all the time, but in this case refers to lunch ladies who come to schools and whip up delicious lunches! It's run by Head Lunch Lady, Saffron Cauliflower. (Much friendlier than the Big G.)

Pick a Pea dance

1. Pick a pea. 2. Pick me. 3. I never liked the garden anyway.

10:40 AM
PUDDLEFORD ELEMENTARY GIRLS' BATHROOMS, MORNING RECESS

I'm glad it's recess, because now it isn't too long until we try Diana's cake, and also we can have a break from singing the silly song about the Queen picking a pea from our school's vegetable patch. (Our class has just finished a rehearsal for *The Princess and the Pea*.)

"Pick a Pea, Pick me!
I never liked the garden anyway!"

As we were leaving the cafeteria, Diana came out of the kitchen. We told her the great news that we'd see her in the line at lunch for some of her famous cake.

24

"I'll look forward to it!" said Diana, smiling.

"I was wondering actually," Violet added, "if I could get your chocolate cake recipe? I'd love to be able to make cake as fluffy as you do."

yum!

Violet

"Oh, sure," said Diana. "I'll be busy at lunchtime, but I've got to go to the supermarket later. Meet me there? About four o'clock?"

"Great!" said Violet, grinning at me and Poppy.

Cool! Most teachers and grown-ups pretend they haven't seen you outside of school, like Miss Twist did at Puddleford Movie Theater last week, but Diana actually wants to meet us. I know it's to give Violet a recipe, but I'm sure it's also because she knows we are totally professional mystery-solvers who have lots of interesting stuff to say.

12:20 PM
LUNCHTIME, PUDDLEFORD CAFETERIA

What we've just witnessed was totally weird.

Everyone was going back to class while the lunch
ladies set up the cafeteria for lunch, so I suggested
to Miss Crumble that Poppy, Violet, and I stay
behind to hang up the vegetable costumes. What
I really wanted to do was make sure we were first
in the school lunch line. It was a good job Miss
Crumble agreed, or we'd have missed the whole
thing.

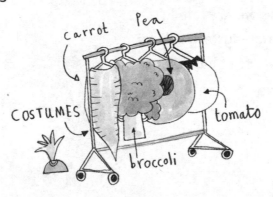

carrot

Pea

COSTUMES

broccoli

tomato

CASE REPORT

mrs. Potter

mrs. Price

mr. Douglas

11:52 AM: Costumes are organized. The lunch ladies and man don't look up from putting out the tables as we walk across the cafeteria.

11:53 AM: As we approach the closed serving station, a loud and distressed-sounding scream comes from the kitchen.

ARGHHHHEEEEEEEEEEEE!

11:54 AM: The lunch ladies and man don't seem to have heard the scream over the noise of tables being dragged, but my Mystery Senses leap into action. Somebody is in need of Mystery Girl assistance!

11:55 AM: We race toward the kitchen, through the door marked "Staff Only." Has Diana's cake exploded everywhere? Is Saffron Cauliflower trapped under a massive can of baked beans?

11:56 AM: The kitchen looks normal. Silver trays of tasty school lunches are lined up by the serving station. Saffron Cauliflower walks out of the storeroom. Spotting us, she looks puzzled. We ask if everything is OK because we heard a scream of terror.

PUZZLED

11:57 AM: Saffron laughs. She says the dishwasher in our school is the most ancient thing she's ever seen. It makes a screaming noise when steam escapes from it. She also says it's nice that we were on high alert, but we aren't supposed to be in the kitchen.

11:58 AM: Violet and Poppy laugh too, and turn to leave. I feel silly, but I notice that we didn't see Diana setting up tables outside and she isn't in the kitchen. I ask where she is.

11:59 AM: Saffron is distracted trying to open the serving window. She says, "Miss Dumpling? Oh, she doesn't work for Ladies Who Lunch any more." Poppy, Violet, and I are all thinking the same thing. WHAT?

12:00 PM: The serving window slides open, revealing a huge line. I quickly ask Saffron why Diana left her dream job. Saffron says not to worry because there will still be a delicious cake today.

12:01 PM: I want to ask more questions, but the other lunch ladies have come in now. Mrs. Price tells us to get out, though not as nicely as Saffron.

NEW MYSTERY TO SOLVE: DIANA DUMPLING HAS DISAPPEARED! WHAT HAS HAPPENED TO HER?

(Violet says that Diana hasn't actually disappeared, she's just stopped working here. But it's a catchy title for this mysterious revelation.)

SIGNS OF MYSTERY: ACTING OUT OF CHARACTER

If somebody you know well begins to act in a manner that is unusual for them (acting out of character), it could be a sign that a mystery situation is unfolding. Can you distinguish between someone who is having a bad day, someone in need of your help—or someone who might, in fact, be a master criminal?

Spotting The Signs:

BECOMING WITHDRAWN: Investigate further if a bubbly person you know seems quieter than normal. Are they being blackmailed about a terrible secret from their past?

Alone

EXCESSIVE TWITCHINESS: Is this person restless because of a guilty conscience? Check news reports for details of terrible crimes. Ask yourself, how well do you know this person?

Twitchy

ACTING IN A ZOMBIE-LIKE MANNER: Sometimes, villainous criminals hypnotize innocent individuals and force them to do their dirty work (jewelry theft, catnapping etc.).

In a trance

IGNORING PHONE CALLS: This may mean that a friend finds you boring. Although, as you are an exciting Young Super Sleuth this is unlikely. Could they have been kidnapped?

Ring, ring

Ring, ring

OVERENTHUSIASTIC LAUGHING: Is this person genuinely amused? Or are they trying to cover up a guilty conscience? Why not track this person's movements to make sure?

Verging on hysterical

WARNING

I know your secret!

We all have days when we don't feel ourselves. If you accuse somebody of being up to no good when, in fact, they just had a bad night's sleep—you may end up with few friends.

YAWN!

12:35 PM
CAFETERIA

Diana Dumpling isn't the only thing to disappear. Her famous cake has too.

It didn't take long for news to ripple down the lunch line that Monday Munchie Madness had been replaced with Princess Pie* dessert and that Diana was nowhere to be seen.

*PRINCESS PIE: Huge pink jell-o mold with green frog prince and crown-shaped candies inside. Impressive but not impressive enough to distract us from what has just happened.

Princess Pie

candies

Saffron told the kids who asked what was going on the same thing she'd told us— Diana doesn't work for Ladies Who Lunch anymore, but that it doesn't mean an end to tasty cakes.

This is so weird. Diana acted like everything was fine when we saw her at break.

"Shouldn't Saffron be more bothered that her star lunch lady is gone? She doesn't even look a bit upset," I said. "And what does `she doesn't work here anymore' even mean? That Diana resigned? Or . . . could she mean Diana was fired?"

"What?! Diana would never do something to get herself fired!" Violet said.

"But, Violet, it doesn't make any sense that she'd choose to leave her dream job either," Poppy said.

"Well, I'm sure Diana will explain everything when we meet her," Violet replied.

Hmmm. Maybe. But would Diana definitely still meet us later—if her day had suddenly gone so horribly wrong? We needed to explore all the logical explanations:

Logical (But Unbelievable) Explanation One:

Diana did something really bad—like cutting her toenails in the kitchen. Saffron was forced to fire her and Diana screamed. Saffron made up the story about the dishwasher and is pretending not to seem shocked because she doesn't want anyone to find out the terrible truth about Diana.

ha ha!

But Diana has studied the Lunch Lady Code of Conduct so she wouldn't suddenly forget lunch lady rules about spreading germs, would she?

toenail germs

Logical (Possible) Explanation Two:

After break, Diana found
out she'd won a
Best Lunch Lady in
the Whole World
competition and
has been whisked
away to write a
school lunch cook
book. The scream
we heard was Diana
with delight. Saffron
made up the story
about the dishwasher
because she is jealous
of Diana's success.

Wouldn't Diana have said something if she'd
entered a Best Lunch Lady in the World
competition? Also, that scream didn't sound
like a happy scream—it was definitely more of
a terrified AHHH! Spider in the bath! sort of
scream.

Spider

(Sort Of) Logical Explanation Three:

Diana realized that she was the best Lunch Lady in the World and decided to leave and set up her own rival lunch lady agency. The scream we heard was Saffron because she couldn't believe Diana would do such a thing.

fuming

But Diana was really happy to get a job at Ladies Who Lunch—would she really want to leave and set up her own company so soon?

VERDICT: We have decided to question Saffron further—she must know what happened and we're not totally sure she was telling the truth about the scream. The lunch ladies usually go home when they've finished cleaning up after lunch, but Saffron does Head Lunch Lady stuff and is sometimes still around until the end of school.

dishwasher

ARRGHEEE!

We located Saffron at the start of break, as she was leaving the kitchen. I explained we are actually detectives, so she should just tell us why Diana doesn't work here any more.

"I've been serving lunch to professional detectives? Wow!" Saffron said. "However, it would go against the Lunch Lady Code of Conduct to discuss the personal matters of my staff. I do have a real mystery you could solve for me though—why is it so hard to get lumps out of custard?"

Saffron being secretive

She winked and strode off. Hmm. Maybe there were rules Saffron had to follow or maybe she was hiding something. But just because she doesn't want to talk, doesn't mean we should give up. (Also, we are capable of solving far more complicated mysteries than why custard is lumpy.)

"Emergency kitchen search needed!" I said.

"I'm not sure about this. We aren't supposed to go in there. Is it really worth getting into trouble when we'll probably see Diana later?" said Violet.

Violet (worried, as usual.)

Until we know for sure the reason Diana left, I think a possible scream and a missing star lunch lady *is* worth getting into trouble for. If we don't search the kitchen now, clues could be swept away and missed forever. I'm going in and I don't care what Violet says! She and Poppy are coming too.

2:40 PM
MISS CRUMBLE'S CLASSROOM

The kitchen was empty. Silver worktops and refrigerator fronts sparkled. My eyes darted around, looking for the ancient dishwasher Saffron had mentioned.

kitchen

empty

I think Poppy was letting the drama of the search get to her. She dashed over to the garbage in the corner, put on a pair of gloves from the Mystery Kit and started shoving garbage covered in slimy school lunch goo into evidence bags.

evidence?

"What?" she said, when I gave her a funny look. "There might be something in here that proves Diana broke a rule. The Young Super Sleuth's Handbook says Garbage Sifting is an excellent way to turn up clues that have been disposed of."

I wasn't sure any of the soggy stuff Poppy was pulling out was going to be useful, but there wasn't time to argue. Saffron could come back at any moment.

I spotted the dishwasher in the far corner, next to the storeroom. I'd been expecting to find some sort of really rusty old machine, but it looked the same as everything else in the kitchen. Sparkling and new. Weird.

sparkling

"Look at this!" Violet shouted, from the other side of the kitchen, by the lunch ladies' pigeon hole.* She was waving a slip of paper.

*PIGEON HOLE: Doesn't actually contain pigeons, it's a compartment with a person's name on it for putting letters and paperwork in.

pigeon

coo coo

I raced over, thinking it might be Diana's resignation letter, explaining why she had quit. Then my tummy did a back-flip because the unbelievable might be true, and what if it was an official letter about her being fired?

"It's Diana's recipe for Munchie Madness Chocolate Cake!" Violet said.

I was a bit disappointed. Finding a recipe wasn't going to tell us anything important. Then I spotted something written at the bottom:

Monday Munchie
Cake Recipe
2 cups flour
3 eggs
3 spoonfuls of honey
Cocoa powder
HEALTHY HIDDEN VEGETABLES
2 cups grated carrot
1 cup grated beet
1/2 cup grated zucchini
Mystery Girls, things are not what they seem.

"Um. What does that mean?" said Poppy.

"It must mean the cake, of course. Chocolate cake is usually unhealthy, but this one is full of vegetables." Violet shrugged.

I'm not sure. I've read lots of stuff in the Young Super Sleuth's Handbook about detectives ignoring clues because they thought they weren't relevant.

"It might mean that, but so far today we've heard a scream that hasn't been properly explained, found out that Diana suddenly doesn't work here anymore, and discovered a cryptic message addressed to the Mystery Girls," I said. "Something definitely isn't right."

"Maybe Diana was planning to give us this note after school, but she had to leave in a rush and forgot it," Poppy said, looking excited.

"I'm sure Diana will be able to clear up this whole misunderstanding when we meet her," Violet said.

I hope so. I'd usually be really excited about a mystery situation like this—I just wish it wasn't Diana who was involved.

Diana's house

5:45 PM
23 PEARTREE AVENUE, DIANA DUMPLING'S
BACKYARD

We waited outside the supermarket for over half an hour, but Diana didn't show up.

If the reason she left Ladies Who Lunch was for something nice, like winning a competition, I'm sure she would have tried to get a message to us.
    Not showing up suggests something bad happened and she's too upset to meet us.

THE SNAPPY SHOPPER

us. Waiting

"Diana is probably fine and just forgot about our meeting because it's been a hectic day," Violet said. "Like the time I forgot we had a Mystery Meeting because I found out I'd been picked to look after the class hamster."

Chip (hamster)

I hope Violet is right. Whatever has happened, we at least want to know Diana is OK —especially if it was her we heard scream. (The dishwasher did NOT look ancient to me.)

Poppy remembered the name of Diana's street, so we decided to go over and see if we could find her. We knocked on a few doors and one of her neighbors told us which house it was. She wasn't home, so we've been waiting outside in case we spot her on her way back.

We've been here for a while now and I suppose there isn't much point in just sitting in Diana's backyard with no idea of when she is due home.

I should probably put the Mystery Kit in the wash too. The evidence in the bags Poppy collected from the kitchen garbage earlier is, as I suspected, just lots of old food and—

yuck!

mystery kit

school lunch leak

GROSS ALERT—one of the bags has leaked school lunch goo all over the Mystery Kit. Poppy!

Before we left, I remembered some advice from The Young Super Sleuth's Handbook about taking logical steps to find out the truth.

"Let's leave Diana a note asking her to get in touch," I suggested.

My mystery notepad was soggy, so I had to use a page from Violet's Kitten Cuddles Weekly Planner. It didn't really look like something a serious investigator would use, but Violet said Diana likes kittens and it might cheer her up if she is in distress.

This is what we wrote:

The Mystery Girls
22 Sycamore Ave

Hi Diana,

We called around to check that you are OK. We were TOTALLY shocked when Saffron told us you didn't work at school any more.

As you know, The Mystery Girls are trained detectives, so if you need our help, or if things are "not what they seem" then get in touch.

Love, Mariella, Poppy, and Violet
x x x

PS: Does the dishwasher at school scream? You might think we are crazy but we are checking it wasn't you who screamed because you need our help.

kitten cuddles

NOTE: Diana hasn't contacted us, yet.
I asked Dad if there had been any
report at the Puddleford Gazette (where
he works) about a lunch lady winning an
amazing prize. So far, nothing. Dad says
he'll let us know if there is.

Tuesday May 19th

Diana — looking distraught

10:40 AM
PUDDLEFORD PLAYGROUND, MORNING BREAK

Before break, our class was rehearsing in the
auditorium again. This was good because it meant
we could keep an eye on the kitchen and listen
for clues, like one of the lunch ladies saying really
loudly, "I can't believe Diana left to set up her own
lunch lady agency" or the dishwasher screaming, or
something like that.

The stage

me

Miss Crumble was getting us to practice our entrance when . . .

ARGHHHHEEEEEEEEEEEE!

The second suspicious scream coming from the kitchen in two days!

"It's the dishwasher! It does scream!" Violet said.

But that noise didn't sound much like steam escaping from a dishwasher to me—it sounded like a very annoyed person.

BANG!

The kitchen door slammed open and the Big G stormed into the cafeteria. A flustered Miss Twist and Saffron Cauliflower followed.

I made an emergency deduction—the Big G had recovered from Lunch Lady's Finger sooner than anyone had thought and she was really angry about something.

"I DO NOT NEED COOKING LESSONS!" the Big G yelled. "ESPECIALLY NOT FROM THAT CAULIFLOWER WOMAN!"

I could see the other lunch ladies gawking from around the kitchen door. (The lunch ladies who had been out with Lunch Lady's Finger were back too.)

miss Twist

Saffron

"Miss Button, we do school lunch the Ladies Who Lunch way now," Miss Twist said. "If you don't like it, I'm sure Saffron is more than capable of running the kitchen."

I thought the Big G might be about to shout something else, but she must have taken Miss Twist's threat seriously because she folded her arms and huffed back into the kitchen.

That explains the scream—it definitely wasn't the dishwasher this time. So what happened yesterday? Operation Surveillance Sandwich* is officially launched.

*OPERATION SURVEILLANCE SANDWICH: Lunchtime is the ideal opportunity to get closer to the lunch ladies (and man) to find out what they know about Diana's disappearance. The Mystery Girls will act like the pieces of bread in a sandwich, closing in on our tasty filling (lunch lady information).

surveillance Sandwich

ARGH! Vegetable mush!

12:50 PM
SCHOOL CAFETERIA, LUNCHTIME

NEW INFORMATION ALERT!

Here are the results of our lunchtime mission to
observe and extract information from lunch ladies
(and a lunch man):

OPERATION SURVEILLANCE SANDWICH:

12:10 PM: Two new Ladies who Lunch ladies
are serving lunch. They are called Mrs. Spooner
and Mrs. Brewster. They tell us they have been
brought in to help teach new recipes to
the Big 6 and
her team.

mrs. Spooner   mrs. Brewster

12:11 PM They are both really chatty—until I ask about Miss Dumpling. They glance at each other, then Mrs. Brewster says very politely that we are holding up the line.

12:12 PM: The Big G flings spoonfuls of lunch onto our plates. She keeps giving Saffron Cauliflower dirty looks.

dirty look

dollop!

NOTE: (Cooking lessons appear to be working, Pirate Pasta Bake with skull and crossbone-shaped pasta and Mango Melt Soufflé are TASTY.)

Pirate Pasta bake

mango melt soufflé

12:35 PM: Saffron starts clearing the table next to us. I decide to use a cunning technique from the Young Super Sleuth's Handbook called Making Innocent Conversation to Draw Out Information.

my innocent face

12:36 PM: I say that we have been looking into the Lumpy Custard Mystery and we should have some answers soon. Saffron is delighted. Now I have her attention I say we'd love to help, because she must be working extra hard getting the new lunch ladies used to our school kitchen now that Miss Dumpling isn't around.

Lumpy Custard

12:37 PM: Saffron beams and says it's sweet of us to worry, but everything is fine and that she meant what she said yesterday—Miss Dumpling leaving is absolutely nothing for us to fret about.

12:38 PM: Before she walks off, Saffron notices we haven't finished our lunch and calls, "Come on, girls! That food won't finish itself. YUM, YUM! IN MY TUM!" (She's always saying that. It's embarrassing—we're not little kids!)

yum yum

12:40 PM: Mr. Douglas (lunch man) is sweeping the floor. As he goes past our table I say I can't believe what I've heard about Diana. (This is another Young Super Sleuth technique called Pretending You Know More Than You Do To Extract Information.)

12:41 PM: Shaking his head, Mr. Douglas says it's terrible that everyone knows and he couldn't believe it when Mrs. Cauliflower told him she had to fire Diana for misconduct. Violet chokes on her cake.

SHOCK REVELATION ALERT ONE: Our worst fears are true! Diana didn't choose to leave— she was fired!

12:42 PM: Mr. Douglas says that Diana must have broken an important rule in the Lunch Lady Code of Conduct to be told to leave immediately. Then he says we are being really nosy, and that, actually, he probably shouldn't be talking to us about it.

12:42 PM: I think quickly and ask if Mr. Douglas has ever heard the dishwasher scream like a crazy person.

12:43 PM: Mr. Douglas raises an eyebrow. He makes a joke about screaming when he has to do the washing up. Then he says since the fancy new dishwasher was installed you can't even tell when it's on because it's so quiet.

SHOCK REVELATION ALERT TWO: Saffron made up a story about the dishwasher and we did hear someone scream yesterday!

VERDICT: The evidence suggests we have solved the mystery of why Diana Dumpling disappeared. She was fired! And the scream we heard yesterday was almost definitely her. I had hoped this wouldn't be true, but now we have proof that it is, I can't get my head around it.

CASE CLOSED

guilty!

2:00 PM
EMERGENCY MYSTERY GIRL MEETING, MISS
CRUMBLE'S CLASSROOM, READING AREA

We are supposed to be having small group practice
sessions for the play, but I can't focus. There are too
many unanswered questions. Like, what is Diana
supposed to have done? Why did Saffron lie about
the scream? Have we really been completely wrong
about Diana Dumpling? And what did she mean in
her note by "things are not what they seem?"

Carrot

beet

zucchini

monday munchie
madness

Things are not
what they seem.

"I'm as shocked as you, but things *are* what they seem," Violet said. "Diana disappeared because she was fired and whatever she did, she didn't want to tell us about it. Saffron fibbed because she was embarrassed that we heard Diana scream. End of mystery."

I know what Violet is saying—the mystery of why Diana disappeared does seem as if it's been solved —but what sort of detectives wouldn't want to get the full story? I want to (and not just because I can't quite believe Diana was fired) because without the details, our final case report would just read: "STAR LUNCH LADY FIRED. Who knows what terrible thing she was supposed to have done? We never bothered to find out."

"The case is solved but it's unfinished," I said. "We don't have all the facts. If we find out the truth, maybe there'll be a way of helping Diana get her job back."

"I don't know, Mariella. You've got a lot of faith in Diana. Not everyone is as amazing and reliable as Violet and I," said Poppy.

I couldn't believe Poppy and Violet were just going to accept they'd got Diana wrong. To me this felt as crazy as hearing your lovely, fluffy old granny was going to prison for a terrible and mysterious crime.

granny

"If I was fired from being a Young Super Sleuth, would you two say, 'Oh dear, we must not have known Mariella very well—we won't even bother to find out what she is supposed to have done'?" I said. (The Young Super Sleuth's Handbook calls this having a highly persuasive argument.)

"Of course you wouldn't," I continued. "You'd get the full story, and that's what we need to do. If we find out Diana was fired for something so awful there's no coming back from it, well, I'll just write that in our case report and accept that I can never trust my Mystery Senses again."

Being able to trust your Mystery Senses is probably the most important part of being a detective, so it would be awful to find out they might have been wrong. I'm sure they're not. I totally would have picked up on it if Diana was a rule breaker.

EXHIBIT A: REBEL DIANA

SECRETLY WILD

not following hair net procedure

grubby fingernails

muck

The Young Super Sleuth's Handbook says not to let the fact you like somebody get in the way of your judgment and I'm totally not doing that. At least, I don't think I am. I just want all the facts. We are going to look for Saffron to tell her we know Diana was fired and she may as well just tell us what for. We are also planning to visit Diana's house again and some of her other known hangouts.*

*KNOWN HANGOUTS: Places you know you are likely to spot a person you are looking for. In Diana's case, we know she often visits Puddleford Library, Loopy Lamb (yarn shop) and the newsstand at the end of Poppy's street where she used to work.

UPDATED MYSTERY STATUS: the disappearing lunch lady is in disgrace— is she washed up or can she sparkle again?

In DISGRACE!

5:45 PM
MYSTERY GIRL HQ

As we were leaving school today, Poppy spotted something that made me think we are totally right to keep investigating.

We've taken this Ladies Who Lunch information leaflet off the parent's bulletin board in the main office.

We already knew Diana was an amazing lunch lady, but none of us knew she'd invented all the Ladies Who Lunch recipes. I'm sure Diana would have been really proud Saffron had given her such a big responsibility—especially when she hadn't been a lunch lady for very long. It makes it even more difficult to believe that Diana would have deliberately done anything to risk her job.

All we know for sure is that it's proving difficult to get the full story.

"I'd love to chat but things are busy, busy, busy!" Saffron said, when we tried to catch her at afternoon break.

Diana was nowhere to be seen at her likely hang-outs and when we went by her house again after school. I tried sending a letter to her mailbox. There was no reply.

Either Diana was out or she was ignoring us. I have to admit, lying low like this does sort of suggest she has a guilty conscience. It's really frustrating.

How are we ever going to get any explanation with Diana hiding away and Saffron and all the other lunch ladies avoiding our questions?

Diana moping in her robe

6:30 PM
MY BEDROOM, 22 SYCAMORE AVENUE

We were trying to decide what to do when Poppy
jumped off the beanbag she was sitting on and
waved the Ladies Who Lunch parent information
leaflet.

"Masters of Disguise training!" she shouted.

I couldn't believe she was suggesting that we have
a Move Like a String Bean Rehearsal instead of
figuring out this case. She didn't mean that, though.

"The leaflet has an address on it for Ladies Who Lunch Head Office!" Poppy said. She was right. I hadn't noticed the small Puddleford address on the back cover.

"We could go there as undercover lunch ladies! There might be a clue to tell us why Diana was fired," Poppy said. "You two are getting really good at being string beans so you could definitely pretend to be lunch ladies."

Violet looked at Poppy as if she was crazy, but this was exactly the sort of genius detective thinking we needed!

"It'll never work—we are way too young to look like professional lunch ladies," Violet said.

"The Mystery Girls are Masters of Disguise," I said. "We can be whoever we want to be!"

It's all planned. Tomorrow after school, we are going to visit the Ladies Who Lunch head office and pretend to be new recruits.

mavis

VERA

Pauline

If we look like we work for Ladies Who Lunch, somebody might totally spill the beans about why Diana was fired. Lunch ladies are much more likely to gossip with other lunch ladies about what's going on.

Poppy said we could have a night off from practicing being a string bean as long as we promised to channel* our inner lunch lady.

*CHANNELING: When you focus your mind on becoming somebody else. I tried to channel my inner lunch lady by wiping the table after lunch. I must have been believable because Mom said it was like there was a totally different person in the room.

me. channeling my inner lunch lady.

DISGUISES: APPEARING OLDER THAN YOU ARE

A true Master of Disguise is able to transform themselves convincingly from an energetic Young Super Sleuth into a much older person. It only takes one childish slip up to blow your cover.

To Look Older You Will Need:

A Gray wig	Fake beard	High heels
A sensible handbag	Fake mostache	Makeup
Fake wrinkles	Shopping cart	Boring socks

To Sound Older, Try Saying the Following:

Oooooh. My back!

My memory isn't what it was.

Years and years and years ago, when I was young . . .

Can you repeat that, please? I'm a bit deaf.

Honestly, I never have a moment to myself.

I don't like rollercoasters, they look so unsafe.

Stylish grown-up neckerchief

Actually aged nine

TOP TIP

Less is more. Using all of these suggestions at the same time may make your disguise unconvincing.

DISGUISES FOR OPERATION DUPE* THE LUNCH LADY:

Lab coats

Platform shoes. To look taller

Hairnets. (shower caps with lines drawn on.)

me, WEARING LIPSTICK

Lipstick.

*DUPE: Tricking somebody into thinking something, like that the Mystery Girls are actually lunch ladies.

Wednesday May 20th

NOTE: The Mystery Kit still needs to be washed. (I had to put it in a laundry bag by the washing machine because the smell was so disgusting.) We are using Poppy's monster backpack as a temporary Mystery Kit.

Temporary mystery kit

LUNCH

Alphabetti Appetizer Pie

Strawberry Surprise Soufflé

12:30 PM
CAFETERIA, LUNCHTIME

Poppy has been really distracted all morning. She's
heard there is a bug going around the sixth grade,
and that both the Princess and the Pea (and a few
other main parts) will need stand-ins if they aren't
better in time for Friday's performance.

She has been humming the Pick a Pea song all
morning, just in case she is asked to audition. I keep
reminding her we need to focus on our plan for this
afternoon instead.

hum
hum
hum
HUM!

Violet thinks the Big G might have persuaded the Puddleford Elementary lunch ladies and man to walk out in protest about the cooking lessons because it's lunchtime and none of them are here. Saffron Cauliflower has taken over on table wiping duty and the new Ladies Who Lunch group, Mrs. Spooner and Mrs. Brewster, are serving.

I'd be surprised if Mrs. Potter, Mrs. Price, and Mr. Douglas walked out because they didn't seem to mind working with Ladies Who Lunch. Perhaps they've all been sent for intensive cooking lessons somewhere?

A few minutes ago Miss Twist and Saffron were having a serious looking discussion by the table, near to where we were sitting.

SERIOUS DISCUSSION

I thought it might be something to do with where the lunch ladies are, or maybe even what happened to Diana, so I tried to listen in. But all I heard was Miss Twist worrying about what school lunch canapés* to serve for parents on Friday.

*CANAPÉS: Finger food served at fancy parties. Miss Twist wants to let all parents know how amazing our school lunches are now so she will be serving Tingling Tomato Puff Pastries and Mini Pirate Pasta Bake Bites.

small

I might have heard something else useful to our inquiry if Poppy hadn't started chair dancing, trying to get Miss Twist to notice her acting talent. Miss Twist shouted at Poppy to act sensibly and walked off. Honestly. I hope she pulls herself together before our mission.

chair dancing

4:45 PM
OUTSIDE THE SNAPPY SHOPPER SUPERMARKET,
CATCHING OUR BREATH

Our visit to Ladies Who Lunch revealed some
TOTALLY unexpected information.

CASE REPORT: OPERATION LUNCH LADY DUPE

4:05 PM: We locate the Ladies Who Lunch
Head Office above the Roll It
Out carpet shop. At
street level, there is a
red door with a small
gold "Ladies Who
Lunch" sign on it.

ROLL IT OUT

Ladies Who
Lunch HQ

4:06 PM: I press the intercom button. Poppy tells us to remember our Masters of Disguise training, but to definitely not get this mixed up with Thinking Like a String Bean, because that will blow our cover.

BUZZ

4:10 PM: The receptionist picks up. Poppy says that we are the new recruit lunch ladies, here for training. There is a click. The door is open.

4:12 PM: Sally (the receptionist) waits at the top of the stairs. I brace myself for her to tell us that we don't look like lunch ladies, but she just says that lunch lady training was yesterday and she wasn't expecting anymore new recruits.

4:13 PM: Poppy replies that we thought training was this afternoon. Then says it's a shame if we're wrong, because our friend, Diana Dumpling, said training was lots of fun. (Argh! Poppy was meant to wait until we'd gained people's trust before bringing Diana up!)

4:14 PM: Sally's eyebrows almost fly off her forehead. (She clearly knows something about why Diana was fired.)

Receptionist

4:16 PM: The receptionist asks us to wait a moment and says that her boss, Mrs. Cauliflower, is in her office and will know what is going on. She leaves the room and the click of her high heels fades away down the hall. Oh no!

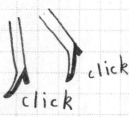

click click click

4:17 PM: Violet is talking really fast about how Saffron will recognize us and we'll get in trouble and we should run. I tell her to breathe. We're not leaving without progressing to Phase Two of our plan. (PHASE TWO: If nobody will talk, conduct a search of the premises.)

4:18 PM: We leap into action. Well, Poppy and I do. Violet listens at the door for approaching footsteps.

FEAR

4:20 PM: I turn around to see that Poppy is shoving garbage into the new monster Mystery Kit backpack, just like she did the other day.

4:21 PM: I'm about to tell Poppy that an apple core is not evidence when she shouts that she has found something—it's Diana's Lunch Lady Employee File! Poppy shoves it into the Mystery Kit.

4:22 PM: Violet squeaks that she can hear footsteps. We hear Saffron saying she definitely hasn't hired any other new lunch ladies. I close the pantry door and give the code word —string bean! (This means make a run for it.)

4:23 PM: We race down the stairs and escape to Puddleford Main Street. I glimpse back and see Saffron in the doorway. She looks confused. Has she recognized us? We don't hang around to find out.

confused

OUTCOME: MISSION SUCCESSFUL.

80

EVIDENCE UNCOVERED

EMPLOYEE FILE

NAME: Diana Dumpling

DISMISSED FOR SERIOUS MISCONDUCT*:
Infringement of Rule 344 of the Lunch Lady
Code of Conduct.

The conduct mentioned here wasn't the only
rule broken but this alone was so shocking
I was forced to skip an Official Warning and
dismiss Diana Dumpling with immediate
effect. By far the worst rule breach I have
ever seen in all my years of being a head
lunch lady.

Saffron Cauliflower

SERVICES
TERMINATED

LADIES WHO LUNCH AGENCY

*SERIOUS MISCONDUCT: Misconduct is when
you do something that goes against all the rules
of your job, which for lunch ladies might be
causing food poisoning or stealing another lunch
lady's handbag.

SAFFRON CAULIFLOWER'S LUNCHBOX: Poppy grabbed it just in case it was important. It isn't. Contains an empty water bottle and some sandwich crusts.

FIVE PAPER CLIPS (ASSORTED COLORS): Poppy found them in the garbage (*Not relevant.*)

EMPTY JUICE CARTON: POPPY!

VERDICT: We still don't know what Diana was fired for, just that it was very, very bad and that she broke more than one rule. This suggests that Diana's career as a lunch lady is definitely over.

NOTE: We have actually broken a Young Super Sleuth Rule! Or Poppy did. Technically speaking, Saffron Cauliflower's lunchbox isn't actually evidence, which means we've stolen it. The lunchbox must be returned as soon as possible.

STOLEN!

S. Cauliflower

5:10 PM
MYSTERY HQ, ANALYZING NEW EVIDENCE

By the time we got back to HQ
we didn't look like Masters of
Disguise anymore. Poppy's
hairnet was as wonky as
my Mystery Senses felt
and Violet had lipstick
smeared across her cheek.

Arthur came running
into the yard. At first I
thought the bright green face paint he was wearing
was another attempt to be a string bean with us. I
was wrong.

"Cool costumes! Do you all have new parts in the play too?" he said. "Miss Twist heard me singing, and guess what? I'm not a potato anymore, I'm the PEA!"

annoying

pea face

Poppy looked horrified. Luckily she's really worried Saffron might have recognized us, so she's managing to focus on trying to decide what we should do about the lunchbox and what we have discovered.

Inside HQ, Violet paced anxiously while Poppy slumped on a beanbag.

"I said we should have closed the case when Mr. Douglas told us Diana was fired!" Violet said. "I don't care about finding out what she did—we are just as guilty as she is for stealing that lunchbox. We have been asking so many questions about Diana, Saffron is bound to guess it was us nosing around her office."

"I'm sure if we just get it back to her she won't report us," Poppy said. (She didn't look very sure.) "At least we know Diana was fired for serious misconduct now. That's enough for our case report, isn't it?"

What? Serious misconduct and the worst rule breach Saffron has ever seen? If I've been *this* wrong about Diana Dumpling, I need to know exactly what she has done, especially because I feel like Saffron must have been talking about Diana's evil twin or something.

Diana's EVIL TWIN!

"We can't give up now!" I said. "There might be a copy of the Lunch Lady Code of Conduct in the school kitchen—we could find out what rule 344 actually is!"

Violet folded her arms, like she was a teacher and totally annoyed.

"Mariella," she said. "We need to drop this before we get ourselves into anymore trouble."

Even though all the evidence is telling me Violet is right, I'm just not ready to accept that I'm a bad detective who didn't notice that Diana had some sort of dark side. I'm not giving up on finding out what rule 344 is yet, even if Poppy and Violet have.

But for now we have to focus on the fact that we might have our careers ruined too—by that stolen lunchbox. We've put this anonymous note inside the lunchbox and we're going to leave it somewhere Saffron will find it tomorrow.

SORRY.
Huge mistake made.
Just returning your lunchbox
that we have cleaned to
make up for it going
missing for a short time.
THANKs!

Thursday
May 21st

Lunchbox stealers

7:50 AM
MY HOUSE, 22 SYCAMORE AVENUE, KITCHEN
TABLE

I hardly slept last night. I kept thinking about what rule 344 of the Lunch Lady Code of Conduct might be and worrying that Saffron had already told Miss Twist we'd stolen her lunchbox.

That's why when Dad came into the kitchen and asked if I'd seen the front page of this morning's Puddleford Gazette, I totally expected to see the headline: LUNCHBOX STOLEN BY FAKE LUNCH LADY MYSTERY GIRLS.

It wasn't that, though. But it definitely explains why there are lots of kids off from school.

PUDDLEFORD GRIPPED BY LUNCH LADY'S FINGER

Puddleford is experiencing an outbreak of the highly contagious Lunch Lady's Finger infection. It is reported that lunch ladies suffering from symptoms, including a rash, flaky skin, and itchiness, have not followed Lunch Lady Code of Conduct hygiene guidelines and the infection has spread from kitchens into classrooms.

There are twelve confirmed cases of children suffering from Lunch Lady's Finger. In addition, there are rumors of a similar situation in ten other schools in the local area.

Penny Parkinson, mother of eleven-year-old Lunch Lady's Finger victim, Primrose Parkinson, shared her reaction:

"My poor princess is missing out on being a real princess in the school play because of unhygienic lunch ladies. Something must be done!"

Miss Twist, principal of Puddleford Elementary, was quick to dispel fears that Lunch Lady's Finger could cause pupil absences to rise to the alarming levels seen during the Itch-in-a-Mug food crisis two years ago.

"The lunch ladies responsible for spreading this illness have been sent home and this morning the whole kitchen was deep cleaned by the Ladies Who Lunch Agency. Saffron Cauliflower and her Ladies Who Lunch have taken over the running of the school kitchen and I can assure you there will be no more cases of Lunch Lady's Finger, only extremely tasty school lunches."

Do you think enough is being done to tackle Lunch Lady's Finger and are your children still going to eat school lunches? We leave you with this word from school lunch supporter, Arthur Mystery.

"It's like our lovely new lunch lady, Mrs. Cauliflower, says, school lunches are yum, yum, yummy in my TUMMY!"

Share your views with us on the usual number 1-800-PUDDLEFORD.

12:45 PM
PUDDLEFORD ELEMENTARY, BACK DOOR OF
SCHOOL KITCHEN

I'm actually pleased Poppy stole Saffron's lunchbox
now! If we hadn't had to return it, we never would
have found out what rule 344 is. (It's nothing to
do with Lunch Lady's Finger either—though after
reading that article, Violet thinks we should be
careful in case we have caught it too.) I'm still in
shock.

Finding the right moment to return the lunchbox wasn't easy. We were stuck in emergency play rehearsals all morning. All other classes have been canceled so that the stand-ins get as much practice as possible. They need it.

Arthur had to call for help halfway through a song because he was stuck under the mattresses on the Princess's bed. His annoying friend Pippa has been cast as the Princess because her sister, Primrose, the original Princess, is sick. Pippa said she knew all the lines from listening to her sister rehearse, but she obviously doesn't.

pea face   pippa

Finally, after lunch, we managed to sneak from the playground to leave the lunchbox outside the kitchen back door.

As we approached,
we heard voices
coming through
the open window.
It was Saffron,
talking to Mrs.
Spooner.

open

Mrs. Spooner   Saffron

I quickly pulled Violet and Poppy behind the big
kitchen wheelie bin. Being caught red-handed with
the lunchbox would be totally embarrassing.

"Don't worry about me," Saffron said. She sounded
upset. "I'm just having a bad week. First I had to
say goodbye to Miss Dumpling, and now all of
those children are ill. I feel bad for Miss Button
and her team—Lunch Lady's Finger is a serious
condition—but they simply weren't following the
Lunch Lady Code of Conduct when they came back
to work while still infectious."

hiding →

Being
nosy

"If anyone can sort this out, you can," Mrs. Spooner said. "I was shocked, though, to hear about Miss Dumpling. Not that I want to pry into your reasons for letting her go."

That was a total lie. It was obvious Mrs. Spooner wanted to know why Saffron had fired Diana as much as I did.

"I probably shouldn't say, but it would be good to talk to someone." Saffron sighed. "You won't believe it when I tell you. Miss Dumpling was planning something completely inappropriate for the Ladies Who Lunch staff party next week."

Poppy and Violet looked at me. Staff party? What was Saffron talking about?

"I'd asked Diana to take care of goodie bags because I thought she would fill them with fun stuff. What she did made me realize I didn't know her as well as I'd thought," Saffron said.

"I found the bags in the storeroom. She was planning to poke fun at the lunch ladies unfortunate condition by putting containers of itching powder in them on purpose!"

SHOCKING!

ITCHY LUNCH LADY

PARTY

"No!" Mrs. Spooner said in disbelief.

"That's what I thought," said Saffron. "Laughing at such a serious issue goes against rule 344 in the Lunch Lady Code of Conduct: Lunch Ladies should take a professional and serious approach to hygiene at all times."

"Oh my! That's such an important rule—what was she thinking?" Mrs. Spooner said.

"I told Diana it wasn't funny," Saffron continued, "but she had a huge tantrum and threw one of the goodie bags at me. Throwing things at other lunch ladies broke yet another rule—rule 225, to be precise. I had no choice but to fire her on the spot."

"I don't blame you!" said Mrs. Spooner.

"I can't let things like that slip," said Saffron. "Imagine if the papers got hold of the story? Nobody would hire Ladies Who Lunch ever again."

Mrs. Spooner and Saffron moved away from the window and we couldn't hear them anymore.

Poppy and Violet gawked at me. I knew what they were thinking. Bad taste goodie bags and tantrums? NO WAY!

I should be happy that we can
finish our final case report,
but I'm not. I can't believe
Diana isn't the person I
thought she was. And I am
totally annoyed with myself
for wanting to believe she
could never have messed up,
even though the Young Super Sleuth's
Handbook said not to let liking somebody get in the
way of the facts.

my mystery senses

Garbage

What was I thinking? I can never trust my Mystery
Senses again.

I feel guilty too. The last thing Saffron needs on
top of Lunch Lady's Finger and Diana's goodie bag
drama is us stealing her things. We left Saffron's
lunchbox by the back door. I hope she finds it.

Poppy says I have to focus on our performance. I suppose there's nothing else to do. BORING!

THE PEA

Friday
May 22nd

I have hung up my
detective hat. Because
I have failed.

7:20 AM
BOTTOM OF THE STAIRS, MY HOUSE

I think I've just found something mysterious, but I'm not totally sure. (Mostly because my Mystery Senses have been so wrong this week that I don't know whether to listen to them or not.)

I was the first one up this morning and I found Watson (amazing pet cat and sidekick) in the kitchen licking something disgusting and slimy.

Watson

A trail of goo led away
across the floor to the
washing machine, where
the bag with the stinky
school lunch Mystery
Kit in still sat. (Mom
was moaning last
night she's been too
busy to do laundry
and that it's Dad's
turn.)

I quickly deduced that Watson had ripped open
the evidence bags of soggy school lunch-covered
garbage and spread them everywhere.

YUCK! I already felt like a bad detective, so I didn't
need to find out the Mystery Kit might now always
smell like school
lunch to remind me of
how I'd got Diana
Dumpling so
totally wrong.

Eau de
Diana
Dumpling

I realized I should probably take the stuff away from Watson, in case cats can catch Lunch Lady's Finger too. I eventually managed to pull a slimy packet out of his mouth.

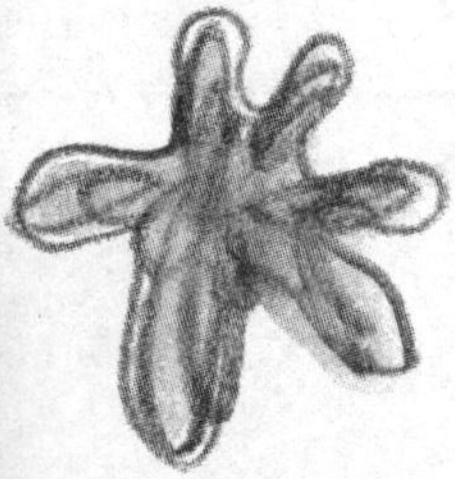

I was about to chuck it in the garbage and wash my hands when something caught my eye.

Now that Watson had mostly licked it clean, I could see what the packet was— a Monster Mash flavored Meal-in-a-Mug, the banned instant meal packet that Arthur is allergic to.

Exhibit A: Monster Mash

MEAL
-in-a-
MUG

MONSTER MASH!

At first I thought Watson had somehow found the multipack at the back of the kitchen pantry, but I've just looked and the box is still unopened.

That means this packet must be from the school cafeteria garbage. WHAT was it doing in there? It definitely doesn't seem like the sort of thing you'd want near school lunches, not when it causes terrible allergic reactions.

It was disgusting, but I knew I should check the other bags of gloopy garbage to see if Poppy had accidentally collected anything else interesting. I rinsed the contents of the bags under the sink . . . and found another strange packet. It was Jelly Jitter Critter flavored Meal-in-a-Mug!

WEIRD ALERT!

Everyone knows not to eat Meal-in-a-Mug after
the Itch-in-a-Mug scandal. Since it's
turned out Diana didn't care
much about the rules,
maybe eating banned
soup is just the sort of
crazy thing she'd do. But
I still don't understand
why she, or anyone else
would want to—not when it
makes you ill.

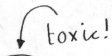

BANNED

Poppy and Violet will probably tell me I should
drop it, but what sort of detective would ignore the
discovery of TWO illegal soup packets of what has
been classed as hazardous foodstuffs in their school
cafeteria garbage?

toxic!

Scenery

PEAS

9:45 AM
PUDDLEFORD ELEMENTARY AUDITORIUM,
FINAL PLAY RUN-THROUGH

Being a detective is so frustrating sometimes—
especially when you start seeing mysteries where
there are none.

There were so many announcements this morning
about everyone being on best behavior when
parents arrive to watch the play that the first
chance I got to talk to Poppy and Violet was when
Miss Crumble told our class to wait on the benches
next to the stage.

Scrambled
mystery
senses

Violet was stressed because Poppy has a lumpy rash on her arms. Mystery Girl with a potential case of Lunch Lady's Finger alert!

Poppy's rash

"I'm fine—I'm sure it's not Lunch Lady's Finger," Poppy said. "My Aunty Pat got a rash because she was stressed and it's been really stressful getting ready for the play and investigating Diana."

"You've caught it from all that stuff you touched in the garbage on Monday!" Violet said, ignoring Poppy. "I bet we've all got it now! You should tell a teacher." She was furiously patting her arms and legs.

"About that garbage Poppy collected," I said. "I think there was something interesting in there."

I told them about the Meal-in-a-Mug packets.

"I love mystery too, Mariella, but there are lots of reasons the packets could have been in the garbage," Poppy said. "A lunch lady probably had them at home at the back of the pantry, like your mom did, and brought them in for lunch without knowing about them being banned."

Maybe. Is it possible not everyone knows about the Itch-in-a-Mug crisis like I thought they did? I suppose somebody who missed all the news stories might not.

"Mariella, those packets need to go back in the garbage—they must be covered in germs!" Violet said. "You probably have Lunch Lady's Finger now too!"

Ugh, I hope not. But I'm starting to think the lack of a real mystery situation has sent me crazy.

me, crazy
and itchy

LOOKING AFTER YOUR MYSTERY SENSES

You may love mystery, but constant detective work can mess up your Mystery Senses, causing you to miss clues and make dodgy deductions. Be constantly vigilant for signs of muddled Mystery Senses and take steps to avoid mystery meltdown.

Exhibit A: Young Detective Suffering from Muddled Mystery Senses

Too afraid to talk to angry clients

Exhausted from late night deductions

Disorganized evidence filing system

Working alone due to arguing with fellow mystery solvers while stressed

Huge pile of unsolved mysteries

Exhibit B: Young Detective with Mind-boggling Mystery Senses

Relaxed and alert

Organized filing system

Appropriate case-load

Supportive mystery sidekick

Ways to Refresh Your Mystery Senses:

Take a long bubble bath

Read a mystery story

Do yoga

TOP TIP

While it's important to take regular breaks it's not advisable to nap in a chase situation in case your suspect gets away.

10:45 AM
AUDITORIUM, PLAY REHEARSALS INTERRUPTED

Unbelievable stuff just happened!

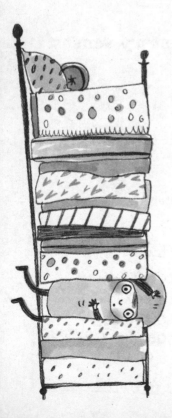

Arthur was on stage, his green face peeking out from underneath a stack of mattresses and blankets. Miss Twist was telling him—again—that he wasn't supposed to be squeaking at this point in the play.

Eeeeeee.Eeeee.

EEEEEEE!

Suddenly, Arthur rolled out from under the mattress and started wriggling around and banging into the legs of the Princess and the Queen. I thought he was channeling his inner pea or something but it was odd, even for Arthur.

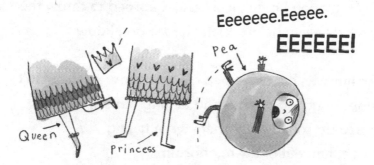

"Get up this instant!" Miss Twist said.

"I can't! I'm itchy! It's itching all over," Arthur squealed.

Everyone on stage backed away. Roberta Poppet shouted that he had Lunch Lady's Finger.

"I don't care what Poppy says. She is infected, and so is Arthur, which means that you probably definitely are too," Violet said. "You need to put those packets in the garbage. NOW!"

"Is that what's going to happen to me?" Poppy said. "This is all Diana's fault! If she hadn't got herself fired, I wouldn't have had to look through the kitchen garbage!"

Even though I didn't feel itchy, I agreed to throw the packets away before Violet had a breakdown.

Arthur was out of his pea costume now and couldn't stop wriggling around and itching himself like a crazy person. The teachers were trying to get him out of the auditorium without touching him. He was being totally dramatic. It was exactly like when he got itchy from eating the Monster Mash Meal-in-a-Mug.

itch

itch

itch

Hmmm.

Hmmm.

But this was Lunch Lady's Finger . . . wasn't it? It couldn't have anything to do with the packets of Meal-in-a-Mug we found in the kitchen . . . or could it?

HANG ON.

The *Puddleford Gazette* article said that the infected lunch ladies were sent home and that Ladies Who Lunch deep cleaned our kitchen yesterday, so there shouldn't be any new cases of Lunch Lady's Finger. But Arthur is itchy and we know for sure Meals-in-a-Mug have been in the kitchen!

DEEP clean?

Wash -○- up

Flaky skin

The Young Super Sleuth's Handbook says that even though coincidences can happen, any slightly suspicious coincidence should be investigated further—just in case.

"I know you'll tell me I'm crazy, but don't you think it's weird that Lunch Lady's Finger has similar symptoms to the itchy reaction caused by the Meal-in-a-Mug crisis?" I said.

Violet looked unimpressed. Poppy raised her eyebrows.

"But, Mariella, in case you haven't noticed, we haven't been served soups in mugs for school lunches," Violet said.

"Meal-in-a-Mug has definitely been in the kitchen, though, and now Arthur, who is allergic to Meal-in-a-Mug, is itchy, even though the kitchen is supposed to have been deep cleaned," I said. "I think we should do another search of the kitchen."

toxic

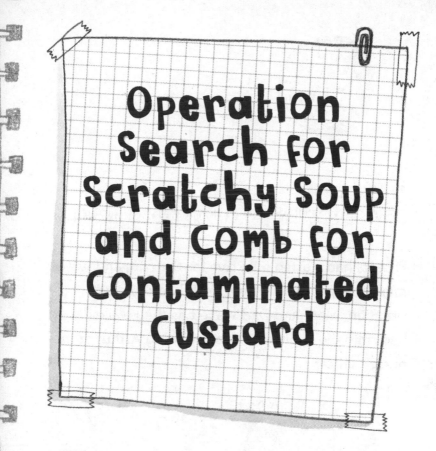

Operation Search for Scratchy Soup and Comb for Contaminated Custard

NOTE: The following events happened so quickly I didn't get a chance to report back at the time.

CAUTION: Do not read further if you are of a nervous disposition. The tension and disbelief will be too much for you to handle.

11:45 AM
SCHOOL KITCHEN, NO LUNCH LADIES IN SIGHT

Parents had started to arrive for the play and were
busy gossiping about the Lunch Lady's Finger
situation. Mom and Dad waved as they walked
back into the auditorium from visiting Arthur at the
nurse's office.

I was beginning to think getting into the kitchen would be impossible, until I saw the lunch ladies had finished carrying trays of fancy-looking canapés to the back of the auditorium and were taking their seats in the back row.

If they were going to be watching the play, that meant the kitchen would be empty. Perfect! We had fifteen minutes before the performance started.

I told Violet and Poppy to follow me and act casual. Nobody noticed us disappear through the swinging door. The kitchen was messier than it had been on Monday. There were bowls by the sink and spilled ingredients. In the serving area were trays of lunches, ready to be served when the parents were gone.

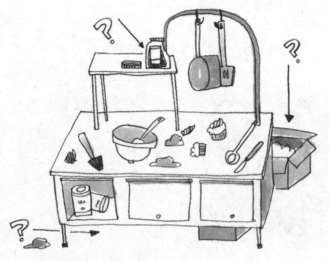

Violet looked under the counters and I checked the pockets of the lunch ladies' coats hanging by the door. Poppy examined the plates and cups neatly stacked on metal shelves. There wasn't a Meal-in-a-Mug packet or granule in sight.

The chatter in the auditorium fell silent and music began. The play had started.

"I knew we wouldn't find anything. Let's just go," said Violet.

"Yeah. We can't miss our big entrance," Poppy said. "This week has been a mystery flop—I don't want our performance to be as well."

I started to get that horrible sinking feeling again that there was something drastically wrong with my Mystery Senses and I'd dragged Poppy and Violet here for no reason.

"Hang on—what's this?" Poppy said from the other side of the kitchen. She was pointing to something.

I moved closer. On the white tiled floor was a trail of red powder with small, uncooked wiggly pasta shapes in it. It looked like the sort of stuff you find in packets of instant soup.

I grabbed the box of Meals-in-a-Mug that I'd brought from home, pulled out the Tingling Tomato Taste Explosion flavor and ripped it open.

"What are you doing? Don't open that—it's a hazardous foodstuff!" Violet said.

I poured some of the packet onto the floor, next to the powder Poppy had discovered. It was the same color and had the exact same tiny wiggly pieces of pasta in it.

"It's Meal-in-a-Mug!" Poppy said.

THE SAME!

12:02 PM
SCHOOL KITCHEN, MAKING AN UNBELIEVABLE DISCOVERY

On closer inspection, I could see that the trail of soup granules stretched toward the corner of the kitchen, under the door of the storeroom.

I ran to the door and pulled it open. The shelves were stacked with giant cans of beans and bags of burger buns, but there was no sign of any Meal-in-a-Mug packets.

Then I spotted something else—lots of jars with little handwritten labels. The scrawly handwriting said they were flavoring mixes for school lunch dishes— Pirate Pasta Bake, Cheesy Chomp, and others we hadn't tried yet.

"The lunch ladies must use these to make all the tasty sauces," Violet said.

I unscrewed the lid on the jar labeled as Pirate Pasta Bake Flavor mix. What I found was totally unbelievable.

The jar was filled with orange powder and skull-and-cross-bone shaped pasta. My heart started to race.

"It's Meal-in-a-Mug! It's been emptied out into this jar!" I said.

"It can't be," said Violet. "It says it's the flavoring for the Pirate Pasta Bake. We ate that skull pasta the other day. It was mixed in with that gooey sauce and vegetables but I remember those pasta shapes."

Violet was right. Of course this wasn't Meal-in-a-Mug.

Unless . . .

multipack box

"What if the Pirate Pasta Bake was made using Meal-in-a-Mug?" I said. "Pass me the multipack box!"

"Mariella, are you OK?" Violet said. "I think the stress of this case is getting to you. School lunches couldn't possibly be made with Meal-in-a-Mug! That would be dangerous."

I flicked through the different flavors, Jelly Jitter Critter Custard, Monster Mash Soup, Noodle Doodle Delight. I pulled out a packet of the Witches' Brew Stew Flavor. Ripping it open, I poured the contents out onto the floor, next to the Pirate Pasta Bake sauce mix.

They were exactly the same color, with exactly the same pasta shapes in them! They just had a different name and the one we'd eaten for school lunches hadn't been served in a mug. It was the same pasta but in a thick sauce with vegetables and cheese on top.

Violet gasped and Poppy clapped her hand over her mouth.

"We should check the other sauce mixes!" I said.

Violet pulled the lid off the
Princess Pie mix.

"It's pink powder with frog
candies in! Oh no. They're
Meal-in-a-Mug granules, aren't
they?" she said.

Poppy ripped open the Jelly Jitter
Critter Meal-in-a-Mug packet and poured
some out. It was the same as the stuff in the jar
Violet was holding. The only difference
was that the jell-o we'd eaten
on Monday had been
made into a huge jell-o
mold.

PRincess
Pie

We opened more sauce
mix jars. They were all filled
with different colored powders that we matched
to the Meal-in-a-Mug granules! But they had been
served with extra ingredients mixed in, so of course
nobody would guess they were eating banned
meals.

This was CRAZY. All our school meals were being made with banned hazardous Meals-in-a-Mug!

SCHOOL LUNCHES!

"This is the reason I've got a rash. I've been eating banned food!" Poppy said, horrified. "You were right about Arthur, and I bet those other kids who are supposed to have caught Lunch Lady's Finger are all just having allergic reactions to school lunches too. Actually, is that what has been wrong with the lunch ladies as well?"

Poppy had a point. I was sure the Young Super Sleuth's Handbook would say it was no coincidence that so many itchy people were in one place.

"If itchy lunch ladies aren't connected to Meal-in-a-Mug I'd be very surprised," I said. "But when the Big G and her team first went home sick they were just serving normal school lunches, so how did they get itchy?"

"I don't know, but I feel itchy, I feel sick, I feel . . . argh!" Violet said.

My head spun with unanswered questions about Lunch Lady's Finger, banned meals—but mostly with thoughts of Diana Dumpling.

We knew she'd done some weird stuff and that she thought itchy lunch ladies were funny. Was she the one behind this? Was this the real, truly terrible reason Saffron fired her? And if that was true, WHY were Meals-in-a-Mug still being served?

DERANGED

LUNCH LADY

EXPOSING A SCANDAL

A scandal is when something shocking and unexpected is revealed about a person or organization. Knowing what to do in order to expose the truth is essential.

Levels of Scandal:

SKELETON IN THE CLOSET: When an upstanding person has been leading a double life and is not who they say they are.

OUTRAGEOUS: When somebody who previously seemed trustworthy, like a teacher, does something wild. Like framing a student for a bad deed.

JAW-DROPPINGLY SHOCKING: When a large number of people are completely fooled by an individual who may have run away with their life savings, or persuaded them to buy fake antique teapots.

Librarian   Criminal

It was him.

$4,000,000 $5,000,000

Fake

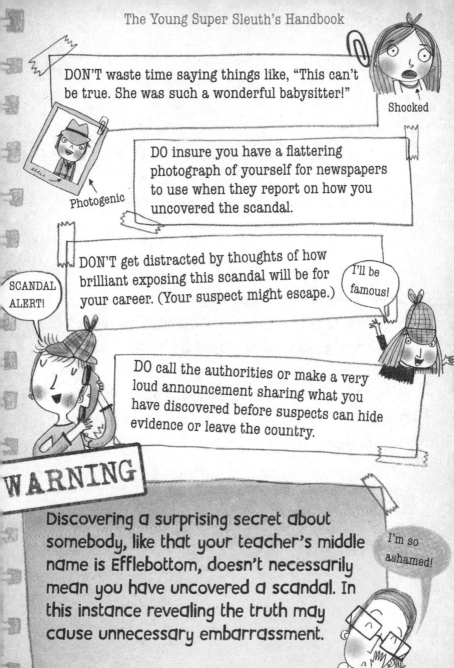

DON'T waste time saying things like, "This can't be true. She was such a wonderful babysitter!"

Shocked

DO insure you have a flattering photograph of yourself for newspapers to use when they report on how you uncovered the scandal.

Photogenic

DON'T get distracted by thoughts of how brilliant exposing this scandal will be for your career. (Your suspect might escape.)

I'll be famous!

SCANDAL ALERT!

DO call the authorities or make a very loud announcement sharing what you have discovered before suspects can hide evidence or leave the country.

WARNING

Discovering a surprising secret about somebody, like that your teacher's middle name is Efflebottom, doesn't necessarily mean you have uncovered a scandal. In this instance revealing the truth may cause unnecessary embarrassment.

I'm so ashamed!

12:10 PM
KITCHEN STOREROOM, IN SHOCK

There was a loud gasp from the audience in the auditorium, as if they knew the terrible thing we had discovered.

"I can't believe Diana was so excited about us swapping to hot lunches," Violet said. "She must have known this is what we would have been eating. She invented every single recipe on Saffron's menu! How could Saffron not know about this? Unless she did and she is covering up to avoid a huge scandal?"

Adding deliberate poisoning to Diana's list of misconducts and realizing there was the possibility that Saffron may have continued to serve toxic food (even though she'd fired Diana for serving it) was a lot to process. Even for my genius detective brain.

"Maybe Diana fooled Saffron like she fooled us. But if Saffron knows about what is really in these jars and she still lets everyone eat it, well, that makes her just as bad as Diana," I said.

"We've got to tell Miss Twist what we've uncovered!" Poppy said, standing up.

I was about to say that yes, we totally needed
to expose the truth—and to stop anyone eating
what must be dangerous Meal-in-a-Mug school
lunch canapés—when I spotted an official-looking
notebook right at the back of the shelf.

"Look at this!" I said. "Maybe it's Diana's secret
recipe book of toxic ingredients."

But it wasn't. On the front was written "Ladies
Who Lunch Weekly Planner, property of Saffron
Cauliflower."

I didn't move for a second because I was busy having a Moment of Suspicion. The planner had been right at the back of the shelf. Had it been accidentally pushed there when the sauce jars were used? Or had it been deliberately hidden so nobody would see it?

"Mariella, we haven't got time to sit around, we've got to warn people," Violet said. "Come on!"

It's a good thing I ignored Violet because as I flicked through the pages I realized that this was most certainly something Saffron Cauliflower did not want anyone to see.

TURN OVER FOR SHOCKING STUFF!

LADIES WHO LUNCH

MONDAY

1. Order fancy plates for school lunch canapés.
2. Write Five Dumpling articles—she knows too much.

TUESDAY

1. Sprinkle Tingling Tomato granules in annoying lunch ladies' uniforms.
2. Order cleaning products. We'll need them when Glenda Button and her team call in to say Lunch Lady's Finger is back! As if!

WEDNESDAY

1. Practice concerned face for when I tell Principal Button woman and her team have Lunch Lady's Finger.

2. Spread rumor Button woman passed her illness to children.

THURSDAY

1. Check on progress infiltrating Sunnyview Elementary.

2. Make up a reason I fired Dumpling to keep everyone from going on about how wonderful she was.

FRIDAY

1. Top sauce mixes with fresh packets of Meal-in-a-Mug. HA!

12:15 PM
STILL IN THE KITCHEN STOREROOM, TRYING
NOT TO PASS OUT

"NO WAY!" Poppy said, grabbing the planner.

"What? Wait. No!" Violet said.

I was grinning. This was the most amazingly useful
bit of evidence we'd found all week. It revealed that
Saffron Cauliflower was the dastardly lunch lady—
not Diana! My Mystery Senses hadn't been short-
circuiting. Diana Dumpling, star lunch lady, really
does exist!

The REAL dastardly
lunch
lady

The happy I-told-you-so feeling didn't last long, though. Not when I thought about how Saffron had fooled us for so long. I could have kicked myself for not being more suspicious of her, especially when she refused to talk to us and we knew she'd lied about the dishwasher.

"What sort of crazy food is this?" Poppy said. "It makes you itchy when you touch it? The poor Big G!"

itch!
itch!
itch!

itch!

"Let me get this straight— nobody has Lunch Lady's Finger?" Violet said. "Saffron just made it look like they did so she could take over school kitchens? But why is she feeding us banned meals?"

I wasn't sure, but what I did know was that with the high levels of unexpected twists and turns in this case, it was probably for a reason we would never guess in a million years. "We still need to figure that out, but at least now we know Diana was fired unfairly," I said. "Maybe Diana knew about Meals-in-a-Mug and was trying to stop Saffron? That must be what she meant by "things are not what they seem" on her recipe!"

"I feel terrible for believing the story about the goodie bags," Violet said.

"Never mind that," said Poppy. "Look at this!"

She was pointing to something on the back of the Jelly Jitter Critter pack.

"Yum Yum in my tum," was written on the back of every flavor, next to the smiling face of TV chef, Arabella Flump, who had been banned from ever cooking for anyone again after the Itch-in-a-Mug crisis. "That's exactly what Saffron says, all the time!"

I said. "Wow, she must have been pretty sure no one would ever guess what she was up to!"

"Hang on. Is Saffron related to that woman on the back of the packet or something?" Poppy said.

I looked at the packet again. Saffron wears different glasses than TV chef Arabella Flump, and has a hairnet. But I could see what Poppy meant—they did look similar, sort of.

SAFFRON CAULIFLOWER

ARABELLA FLUMP

"Sorry to interrupt you, but what exactly are you doing in my storeroom?" a voice behind us said.

nasty cauliflower

12:20 PM
SCHOOL KITCHEN, FACE TO FACE WITH A
CUNNING CAULIFLOWER

It was Dastardly Lunch Lady Saffron Cauliflower!
She was smiling, and the weird thing was that she
didn't look even a bit angry we'd uncovered her
shocking secret.

I was about to say the sort of thing
a genius detective would
say, like "You can't pull
the dirty dishcloth over
our eyes anymore,
Saffron!" But Poppy
beat me to it.
"You! You gave me a
rash!" she screamed.

Argh! Cauliflower

140

"You've made a lot of people ill! Well, we know about the special secret ingredient you've been putting in our school lunches!"

Saffron kept on smiling, but her eyes flashed to the mess of granules and Meal-in-a-Mug packets on the floor.

"Yeah, and I know secret ingredients are meant to stay secret, but there's no way we are keeping this quiet, Cauliflower," I said.

It felt really good calling Saffron by her last name. I hoped that would annoy her and make her finally drop the stupid Fake-Delightful-Lunch-Lady act.

"Pick a Pea, Pick me!
I never liked the garden anyway!"

The sound of singing came from the auditorium. It was almost time for us to be on stage.

Poppy looked more furious
than ever. I didn't blame
her. Not only did she
have a rash, but Saffron
was messing up our big
entrance in the play.

POPPY
fuming

"I'm sure I don't know what you
mean," Saffron said. "Now, I think we need to clean
up this mess you've made. Don't you?"

Poppy and Violet looked at me, unsure what to
do. Thinking quickly, I used a technique from the
Young Super Sleuth's Handbook called Creating a
Distraction.

"Look, Miss Twist is here. She can help you clean
the pantry," I said, gesturing toward the kitchen
door.

It worked. Saffron spun around.

"RUN!" I shouted.

12:25 PM
SCHOOL AUDITORIUM, CARRYING HAZARDOUS
FOODSTUFFS

BANG!

Poppy pushed open the kitchen door so hard it
bounced off the wall. All the parents turned to
see three string beans racing out of the kitchen.
Glancing behind, I saw Saffron had stopped in the
doorway. She seemed undecided whether to chase
us or attempt to dispose of the evidence in the
kitchen.

running
beans →

Mom took a photo
and gave me the
thumbs-up. Some
of the other parents
smiled too. Arthur's
friend, Pippa, stopped
dancing with the empty
pea costume on stage and
stared at us. Miss Twist
was furiously pointing at the benches
where we were supposed to be sitting.

The Young Super Sleuth's Handbook says to always
carefully prepare a speech and to appear calm
before making public announcements. So escaping
from a deranged lunch lady while dressed as a
string bean wasn't the most ideal way to reveal
what we'd uncovered, but we couldn't wait and risk
Saffron moving the evidence.

"Saffron Cauliflower has been feeding us all banned
Meals-in-a-Mug—the stuff was a big scandal about
two years ago that made everyone itchy!" I shouted.

It was supposed to come out in my serious detective voice, but instead it came out in sort of a rush and very high-pitched.

To my surprise, nobody looked as horrified as I thought they would. They just seemed confused and as if they thought I should sit down if I wasn't going to sing a nice song. Mom and Dad were both blushing bright red.

Embarrassed

"Mariella Mystery, I am shocked," Miss Twist said finally.

Great! I thought. This is a huge school lunch scandal, so you should be. But she wasn't talking about the school lunches.

Not happy

"I expect this sort of show-off stunt from Poppy Holmes, but not you and Violet Maple," she continued.

Parents were looking away now, raising their eyebrows and muttering. Mom was pretending she didn't know me.

"Don't be too hard on them," Saffron said. "I think our super school lunches must have given them super-powered imaginations. Of course, performing will only make them more overexcited. The best thing would be for them to wait with me in the kitchen until the play finishes."

Super-powered imaginations? What nonsense. There was no way we were going with her.

itchy brain

"We've got evidence! These jars are filled with banned Meals-in-a-Mug!" I said. "And if you look in the kitchen, the storeroom has even more!"

evidence

Whispers rippled through the auditorium. Did anyone believe us?

"Enough!" Miss Twist shouted.

"Yes, come on, girls, don't spoil the play anymore than you already have," Saffron said.

Violet hid behind my shoulder. Poppy backed away. The Young Super Sleuth's Handbook says that if nobody believes your accusations, you may as well have not bothered solving the mystery because your reputation will be ruined forever. This was a disaster.

Then . . .

BANG!

The door leading to the main office was flung open.

Standing in the doorway, red-faced and windswept, was the Disappearing Lunch Lady—Diana Dumpling!

Diana!
(still wearing her hairnet.)

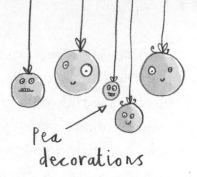

Pea
decorations

12:30 PM
SCHOOL AUDITORIUM, WITH A DISAPPEARING
LUNCH LADY

Diana's eyes immediately flashed to the jars of
Meals-in-a-Mug that Poppy, Violet, and I were
holding. I could tell she knew we had figured it out.

"What the Mystery Girls have said about the
Cauliflower woman is true!" Diana said to the
shocked faces in the auditorium.

This was the Diana Dumpling we knew, with some
added Mystery Girl attitude! Where had this come
from? And why now?

"Saffron Cauliflower has tricked you into thinking her school lunches are the best around, just like she tricked me into believing I was creating recipes that used vitamin-enriched powdered vegetables!" Diana shouted. "I've been too afraid to speak out because she threatened to tell everyone it was all my idea . . . until I realized I'd feel guilty forever if I let this continue. I'm too late to stop innocent children from eating dangerous food, but I can stop parents from falling ill from eating those canapés!"

Go, Diana!

"You all deserve to know the truth about how lunch ladies in this school—and in others—have been made to look as if they have an unhygienic illness when they don't," Diana continued. She fixed her eyes on Saffron. "None of those lunch ladies deserved to have toxic soup granules put in their uniforms!"

Parents in the audience
looked really confused now.
The lunch ladies sitting in
the back row were staring
at Diana in disbelief. Saffron
had turned a funny shade of
purple.

PURPLE

"Do not listen to this woman,"
Saffron said. "I had to fire her for serious
misconduct. She was making fun of the poor Lunch
Lady's Finger victims and she threw a goodie bag
at me!"

"FIBBER!" Poppy screamed, grabbing Saffron's
planner off me and waving it in the air. "That's a
total lie and we've got proof!"

Miss Twist was gazing from Saffron to Diana.

"Saffron Cauliflower is not the lunch lady you think
she is, and I can prove it," Diana said, folding her
arms.

"Can't I, Saffron? Or should I say ARABELLA FLUMP, disgraced TV chef and maker of the only instant meal products ever to be banned because it can cause horrible symptoms, like uncontrollable itching!" Diana continued. "At least her terrible mug creation was mixed in with other ingredients to disguise it, or the symptoms being suffered by children would be just as bad, if not worse, than during the Itch-in-a-Mug scandal."

WHAT? Saffron was Arabella Flump? Of course!

ARABELLA
FLUMP-i-Flower!!!

The whole auditorium gasped so loudly I felt like air should be rushing past my face. They believed Diana! (Maybe me breaking the news to them dressed as a string bean had made it hard for them to take seriously.)

"I am Saffron Cauliflower. I make delicious school lunches!" Arabella shouted.

She looked desperately at the cast of *The Princess and the Pea* gathered around the stage.

"Don't I, children? What do we always say about school lunches?" she beamed and rubbed her tummy. "Yum yum in my tum!"

What? She'd totally given the game away herself now! HA!

yum
yum
in my
TUM!

"Funny you should say that, Saffron Whoever-you-are," I said. "That's exactly what you wrote on the back of Meal-in-a-Mug packets."

Violet and Poppy held up the evidence so everyone could see. Miss Twist grabbed one of the packets and stared at it.

Mrs. Spooner leaped from her seat and yanked off Saffron's hairnet. Tons of blonde curly hair tumbled out. Saffron did not look like Saffron anymore—she looked like Arabella Flump. (Because that's who she really was.)

"She tricked us! She's tricked us all!" Mrs. Spooner shouted.

Everyone was now looking at Saffron (or Arabella) in disgust.

"Mrs. Cauliflower, I mean Flump. Or whoever you are, get out of my school—immediately!" Miss Twist said angrily. "The Ministry of School Lunches will be hearing about what you've done!"

Mr. Muffet, the second grade teacher, and Miss Crumble got up and started to escort Arabella out of the auditorium.

HORRIFIED!

"I don't know what you're making such a fuss about. Your kids have been eating my Meals-in-a-Mug for weeks thinking they're delicious, because they are!" Arabella shrieked. "Only a few of them got itchy! And the lunch ladies I got rid of were no good anyway!"

Mr. Muffet pulled on Arabella's apron. Miss Crumble pushed her toward the door.

"How you ever called yourself a children's chef, I do not know!" Diana said, as Miss Crumble and Mr. Muffet give Arabella a final shove out of the auditorium.

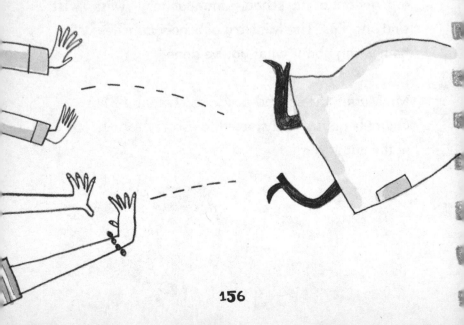

Wow. Diana had totally stood up for herself! She is the best expert witness we've ever had in an investigation! (It took her a while to come forward, but after what she's been through, I think we can let her go.)

"A bit of itching never hurt anyone!" Saffron screamed, her voice fading away down the hallway. "Your kids would have gotten used to the food **EVENTUAAAALLLLY!**"

There was a stunned silence.

Then Arthur's friend Pippa's mom started to clap. "Hooray for the Mystery Girls!" she yelled. "Without them whole families could have ended up itchy! And hooray! My daughter Primrose isn't suffering from a highly contagious disease, she is just having an allergic reaction!"

So happy she could cry

There were whoops and cheers from the other parents, and the Ladies Who Lunch and everyone on stage. And lots of clapping. Mom was proudly telling the woman next to her I was her daughter.

"You don't need to thank us," I said, as the noise calmed down. "It was all in a day's work for the Mystery Girls, and some assistance from a key witness star lunch lady, Diana Dumpling, always helps."

There was more clapping and Diana blushed. Poppy and Violet hugged me and started jumping up and down, which felt amazing, but made it hard to say my closing line. (It's always good to say something interesting when you have solved a case so that people think you are even more clever than they already do.)

"Now may I suggest, the show must go on!" I said. (Really I wanted to stay and listen to everyone tell us how great we are, but the Young Super Sleuth's Handbook says that detectives shouldn't soak up the praise too much or everyone will think you are just in it for the glory.)

"I would also like to issue one last piece of Mystery Girl advice. Do not eat those canapés—you might get very itchy indeed," I said.

"Definitely," said Diana, "I'll make you some fresh ones, without any suspicious ingredients at all!"

Everyone clapped and whooped again. I probably should have stopped them, but a little more celebration never hurt anyone!

Saturday
May 23rd

Garbage

11:00 AM
MYSTERY GIRL HQ, EATING LEFT OVER MONDAY
MUNCHIE CAKE. YUM!

I'm still grinning just as much as I was yesterday
because we managed to get the full story about
Diana Dumpling and we totally exposed the biggest
school lunch scandal EVER.

When Arthur was released from the nurse's office, he tried to hug me while everyone was looking. I did not look cool and professional with an itchy, squeaking pea hanging off me. But we'd proved that Arthur was having an allergic reaction, and wasn't actually contagious, so he was allowed to come back and play the part of the Pea.

I'm glad I don't seem to be allergic to Meals-in-a-Mug because the itchiness looks really awful. Poppy's rash is almost gone now, but she had a lucky escape. Meals-in-a-Mug affect people in different ways depending on how bad their allergy to it is.

Poppy was lucky just to have a rash, but if she had eaten more Meals-in-a-Mug her symptoms may have gotten worse and she would eventually have ended up in the same state as Arthur or some of the kids who were off from school.

vomit

If Saffron hadn't disguised Meals-in-a-Mug as school lunches, with added ingredients like vegetables, pastry crusts, and cheesy toppings, the Mystery Girls would have figured the whole thing out far sooner.

mild allergy

We got another really big cheer when we made our entrance as string beans. I'm not sure true Masters of Disguise would do this, but we did come out of character and make a little bow to the audience.

Best BEANS ever

Diana organized the other lunch ladies to whip up some tasty new school lunch canapés. She made a huge batch of Monday Munchie Madness chocolate cake too, even

PEa garnish

yummy

though it was a Friday, and it totally does taste like a cloud of chocolate melting in your mouth.

I got sad when the play was over and lunch had finished, because now that we knew the Big G and the other lunch ladies didn't really have Lunch Lady's Finger, it meant that Diana Dumpling wouldn't work in our school anymore.

But we got some amazing news when Miss Twist announced that she wanted to offer Diana a job as Lunch-Lady-in-Charge of Recipe Development!

Diana looked as if she might cry with happiness when it happened—and she said yes, as long as Miss Button (The Big G) agreed to it when she returned.

DElighted

The police are investigating Arabella Flump in partnership with the Ministry of School Lunches. They have been speaking to the lunch ladies who had Meals-in-a-Mug used against them and plan to charge Arabella with Food Crimes of an Itchy Nature.

They've never seen a case like it, and Arabella might even go to prison. (Apparently she has already been told she won't be allowed anywhere near the kitchens there.)

All of Puddleford knows about the case of the Disappearance of Diana Dumpling. Wherever we go, we get clapped! I haven't had a chance to write up the whole story, until now.

CASE REPORT: THE DISAPPEARANCE OF DIANA DUMPLING

Diana Dumpling didn't actually disappear. She went into hiding after being fired from the Ladies Who Lunch Agency because she had discovered the terrible truth about the sinister ingredient being used to make school lunches.

Saffron Cauliflower was actually Arabella Flump, the celebrity children's chef, whose reputation was ruined after a scandal surrounding her line of instant Meals-in-a-Mug products, which caused severe itching and vomiting in children.

Arabella
"Itch-in-a-Mug"
FLUMP

Convinced the
itching scandal
was a lot of
fuss about
nothing, and
with a celebrity
lifestyle to fund,
Arabella combined
her knowledge of cookery
and her huge supply of banned Meals-in-a-
Mug to terrible effect. She decided to disguise
and sell the packets to a new, unsuspecting
market—school lunches.

↑ Arabella's mansion

Arabella set up Ladies Who Lunch and became
Saffron Cauliflower. She emptied the Meals-in-a-
Mug into large jars and re-labeled them as food
flavoring mixes. None of the lunch ladies she
employed guessed that they were actually using
banned meals in their school lunches.

flavoring
mixes ←

One afternoon, Diana walked into Arabella's office without knocking and discovered her without her hairnet on, emptying Meal-in-a-Mug packets into jars. Everyone knew Arabella Flump had been banned from cooking for people ever again, and using ingredients that would make children ill went against all Diana's Lunch Lady Training.

Arabella told Diana that if she breathed a word, she would make everyone believe that Diana had known about the ingredients when she developed her school lunch recipes. Terrified that her lifelong dream of a career as a lunch lady would be ruined, Diana continued to work for Arabella for a number of weeks after her shocking discovery.

Arabella was able to infiltrate Puddleford
Elementary as well as ten other elementary
schools by making existing lunch ladies believe
they were suffering from Lunch Lady's Finger.
Lunch Lady's Finger is a real illness, but it
wasn't what was making the lunch ladies
sick. Arabella had sent them new uniforms
contaminated with undiluted Meal-in-a-Mug
granules.

The packages were falsely marked as being from
the Official Ministry of School Lunch Uniform
Department. Because they weren't diluted with
water or anything else at all, the granules acted
as powerful itching powder, causing a bad
rash within minutes of
coming into contact
with skin.

After consuming school lunches containing Meals-in-a-Mug, some children who were especially sensitive to the mixtures' banned contents began to fall ill with severe itching. Nobody suspected in a million years they were eating Meals-in-a-Mug, so the finger of blame was pointed at Lunch Lady's Finger and unhygienic lunch ladies.

itchy finger of blame

Arabella was sure that children would become less itchy once they were used to school lunches, allowing her to make a fortune while getting rid of her stash of Meals-in-a-Mug. She thought if she made the existing lunch ladies look bad, she would be able to steal their jobs permanently.

Arabella's school lunch fortune

On Monday, Arabella realized Diana had been making Monday Munchie Madness cake without using Meal-in-a-Mug granules. When Diana tried to stand up for herself, Arabella decided she couldn't be trusted and fired her.

As she was being thrown out of the kitchen, Diana screamed. The Mystery Girls heard this and thought it was highly suspicious. What Arabella didn't know was that Diana had been planning to tip us off after school with a note saying "things are not what they seem."

Diana had planned to write more but she was forced to leave before she could finish. After she lost her job, she was so upset, worried, and confused that she ignored our attempts to contact her.

Diana in bed

Arabella attempted to throw everyone off the scent of what had really happened by making up a terrible story about Diana and bad taste goodie bags.

Fortunately evidence emerged allowing us to link Ladies Who Lunch to the outbreak of fake Lunch Lady's Finger in lunch ladies and children to their school lunches—two packages of Meals-in-a-Mug discovered in the kitchen garbage.

With so many schools to supply Arabella got sloppy, just like one of her mug-based snacks. Ha!

SLOPPY

CASE CLOSED.

NOTE: We are still trying to persuade our principal, Miss Twist, that the Mystery Girls should be entitled to a free pass to the front of the line as a reward for our school lunch saving skills. She said we were pushing our luck.

173

Three beans and a STAR lunch lady!

ACKNOWLEDGMENTS

I'd like to say a big thank you to the wonderful people who have helped me develop *The Disappearance of Diana Dumpling* and the rest of Mariella's mysteries. Firstly, a standing ovation for my editor and honorary Mystery Girl, Jenny Glencross, for her wonderful ideas and keen mystery solving mind. A huge *totally* amazing whoop for everyone at Orion for getting behind Mariella and for helping to spread the word of the Mystery Girls far and wide. And lastly a huge round of applause for my husband, Simon, as a reward for listening to me talk mystery so much he can be a Mystery Girl too, if he likes.

Kate Pankhurst, May 2015